MW01043676

10 GREAT JEWISH CHILDREN'S STORIES

◆

BY CHAYA BURSTEIN

ILLUSTRATIONS BY AMY & MIRIAM

PITSPOPANY PRESS

ST. HELIER, JERSEY

Copyright © 1994 Illustrations and Design by Amy Ross & Miriam Shpira
Copyright © 1994 Stories by Chaya Burstein
All rights reserved.
ISBN #9-654-83005-1
Printed and assembled in Hong Kong.
Magnifying glass made in USA.

TABLE OF CONTENTS

Ready for some fun?

Use your handy magnifying glass to look at the different characters below. Try to remember what they look like.

Then, after you read a story, turn the page. You will find a colorful illustration of that story. See if you can spot all the hidden characters scattered throughout the picture.

If you have trouble remembering what the characters look like, turn back to this page.

JACOB AND THE HAUNTED SUCCAH

◆

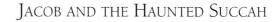

etrog

lulav

candles

THE ANGRIEST BEST FRIEND

◆

pomegranate

shofar

tallit

MRS. MACCABEE WINS THE BATTLE OF HANUKKAH

◆

dreidle

menorah

oil lamp

latke

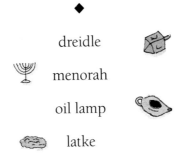

A PURIM THANK-YOU DISH

◆

hamantaschen

Megillat Esther

grogger

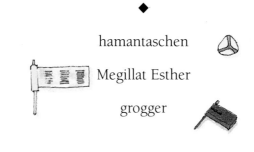

THE LITTLE LOST TREE

◆

cherries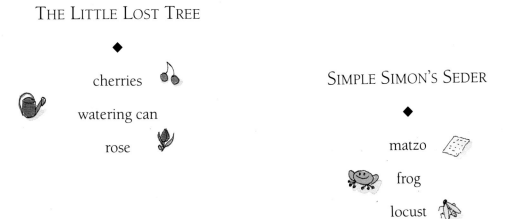

watering can

rose

SIMPLE SIMON'S SEDER

◆

matzo

frog

locust

A BIRTHDAY PRESENT FOR THE TORAH

◆

Torah scroll

cheese

apple

THE CURIOUS QUEEN

◆

rattle

mezuzah

present

IN FARAWAY PLACES

◆

9 number nine

sad face

trumpet

MUTTLEY'S FIRST SHABBAT

◆

gefilte fish

challah

siddur

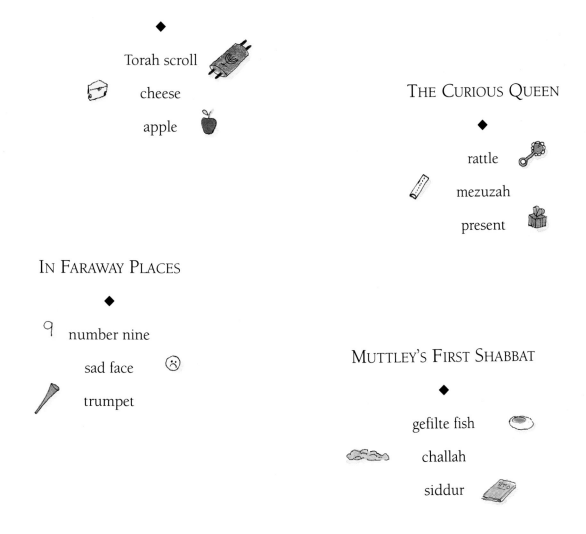

Have fun!

THE ANGRIEST BEST FRIEND

Sandy and Jan walked to school together and played Barbie dolls together. They did homework and rode bikes together.

But one morning when Sandy called for Jan, she had already gone to school. When Sandy got to the schoolyard Jan was playing jacks with Karen. She didn't say hello—she didn't even look up! During recess, when Jan was captain of her dodgeball team, she didn't pick Sandy. And when school was over, Jan packed her schoolbag and skipped home alone. She didn't look around once.

"She must be mad at me," thought Sandy. "But why? She's my best friend. I'll ask her." Sandy rode her bike to Jan's house. Jan was sitting on the front steps holding her big fluffy cat.

"Wanna play?" called Sandy. Jan tucked her nose into the cat's fur and turned away. Sandy got angry. "If you won't talk to me I won't talk to you," she shouted. Then she wheeled her bike around and rode home.

After that, Sandy went bike riding with Randi from next door. But it wasn't as much fun. She played Barbie dolls with her little sister. But her sister tore Barbie's evening gown. And she did homework at the kitchen table—alone.

"Where's Jan?" her mother asked.

"Who cares!" answered Sandy, and then she started to cry. "She's mad at me, so I'm mad at her. But I don't know why we're mad at each other," she sobbed.

Sandy's mother looked sad. Then suddenly she began to smile. "I know what you can do," she said.

"There's nothing to do," insisted Sandy. "She's stupid!"

"She's your friend," her mother reminded her. "Your best friend. And I know something you can do to keep your friend. Do you remember which Jewish holidays are coming soon?"

"Rosh HaShanah and Yom Kippur. So what," Sandy mumbled.

"We do a special thing in the days between Rosh HaShanah and Yom Kippur," Sandy's mother told her.

Sandy wiped her eyes. "What do we do?"

"We go to our friends and family and we say, 'If I did anything to get you angry or hurt your feelings during this year, please forgive me.'"

"Uh-uh!" Sandy shook her head. "I will *not* say that to Jan. I didn't do anything!"

"Maybe she thinks you did. Try."

"No!" Sandy picked up her books and stomped out of the kitchen.

Soon it was Rosh HaShana. Sandy didn't go to school. She and her family got dressed in holiday clothing and went to the synagogue. And there, two rows behind them, sat Jan and her family. Jan and Sandy looked at each other. They both had long, sad faces.

"Try," Sandy's mother whispered.

Sandy got up. Jan got up. They met in the aisle. "Jan," Sandy began slowly, "if I did or said anything to get you mad at me, please forgive me."

"You did!" Jan declared angrily. "Karen told me that Shelley told her that you said that I was a big fat brat!"

"I did not!" Sandy cried. "I never said that! I said you have a big fat cat."

"Oh," Jan gasped. Her face lit up and she smiled. Sandy smiled too. Then they held hands and began to giggle.

"Shhhhh!" Everyone in the synagogue turned around and scolded.

"Quiet, please!" declared the rabbi as he looked up sternly from the pulpit.

Sandy and Jan held their breath and covered their mouths, but they couldn't stop giggling.

They were so glad to be best friends again.

DO YOU KNOW THAT:

◆ Rosh HaShanah is the Jewish New Year.

◆ There is a custom to dip challah in honey on Rosh HaShanah for a sweet New Year.

◆ The Shofar, a ram's horn, is blown on Rosh HaShanah. The horn's sound reminds people to wake up and start thinking about the really important things in life—like helping people and listening to parents.

◆ Ten days after Rosh HaShanah is Yom Kippur. On Yom Kippur Jews don't eat or drink—they fast—the whole day. They pray in synagogue, asking God to forgive them their sins.

◆ Little kids don't fast all day on Yom Kippur. Sometimes they wait an extra hour or so in the morning before eating breakfast. That's considered fasting too.

FIND:

pomegranate 2
shofar 2
tallit 1

שנה טובה!

JACOB AND THE HAUNTED SUCCAH

Flashlight!" snapped Joel, as he checked off the list of things they wanted to bring with them."Got it," said Noah, his best friend.

"Candy!"

"Got some," Noah answered.

"Sleeping bags!"

"Right here," declared Noah, pointing to the sleeping bags piled in front of them.

"Then we're ready to go and sleep in the succah," announced Joel.

"Can I come too?" asked Joel's younger brother Jacob.

"No way! It's too dangerous. There are wild animals out there," Joel told him. "You'd be scared."

"I wouldn't. I promise. Please?" Jacob pleaded.

"You'd cry and we'd have to take you into the house," Joel insisted. "Forget it."

Jacob stood at the window and watched Joel and Noah go into the backyard. He was jealous. And he was angry. Suddenly he had an idea. He grinned from ear to ear.

As soon as it got very very dark, Jacob took the ladder out of the garage, the broom out of the kitchen, and a white pillowcase from the linen closet. Then he tiptoed into the backyard—where the succah stood—and filled the garden watering can.

It was dark and quiet in the backyard. Jacob was scared, but he wouldn't give up. He was too angry.

Three curious cats jumped off the fence and followed him to the back of the

succah. Jacob took a long, deep breath. Then he cupped his hands to his mouth and howled as loudly as he could. "AAAAAHOOOOOOO!"

Inside the succah, Noah opened his eyes and sat straight up. "W-wh...what was that?" he asked, shaking Joel. "Was that a wolf?"

"No," Joel assured him. "It's just a dog. Don't be scared. Go to sleep."

"AAAAHOOOOOO!" Jacob howled again, louder. This time the neighbor's dogs woke up and they howled too. The cats hid under the pillowcase.

"Those aren't dogs," Noah insisted. "Those are wolves! Big wolves! I'm going inside."

"Stop being such a baby," Joel told him. "They're just my neighbor's dogs. They'll stop howling in a minute."

And sure enough they did.

Soon Jacob heard Joel and Noah breathing deeply. He knew they had fallen asleep again. He carried the watering can and climbed up the ladder to the roof of the succah. Two squirrels woke up and crept down onto the roof to watch him. Jacob tipped the can and let it drip on his brother's head first and then on Noah's head.

"Fffflmph...achooo!" Noah sneezed and woke up. "Hey—it's raining! Joel, c'mon wake up! It's raining."

Joel opened his eyes and looked up. "The stars are still out. It's just the morning dew," he yawned. "Zip the bag over your head until it stops."

"Achooo!" Noah sneezed again. Then he tucked his head into the bag.

Jacob climbed down the ladder. He put the white pillowcase on top of the broom. Then he tiptoed around to the doorway of the succah. The cats followed him. When they smelled the candy they scooted inside.

"OOOOOH WOOOO!" Jacob moaned, making his voice sound as deep as he could. He waved the broom.

This time Joel woke up first. "Noah, look!" He poked his friend. "What's that?"

Noah rubbed his eyes and looked up. "AIYEEE! It's a ghost!" he yelled, springing out of the sleeping bag. In the dark he stepped on the tail of one of the cats.

"Yeowrrr!" screeched the cat. "Meow!" cried the other cats. They scrambled around the succah trying to get out.

The squirrels chattered excitedly on the roof. "Ch-ch-ch".

"OOOH WOOO!" Jacob moaned again.

"OUCH! OOCH! EECH!" Noah and Joel shouted as they bumped into each other and the poles of the succah.

With a startled "Ch-ch-ch" the squirrels fell through the roof and plopped onto the sleeping bags.

"YEOWRRR...MEOW...OUCH...EECH... OOOOOH...WOOOOO...C-CH-CH..." The dark little succah rocked with noise.

Suddenly a bright light went on. Joel and Jacob's parents stood in the doorway of the succah holding a flashlight. The cats and squirrels scrambled out between their legs.

"Did you invite all these cats and squirrels into the succah?" Joel's mother asked.

"No, we sure didn't," Joel told them. "And for sure we didn't invite **him**." He pointed to Jacob who was still holding the ghost-broom.

"Well, you should have," his father said. "On Succot we invite our Torah relatives, like Abraham and Sarah, Isaac and Rivkah, and...."

"*Jacob*, Rachel and Leah," Jacob finished.

"Exactly," his father said. "You should have invited Jacob too."

"But he's a just little kid, Dad! He would just get scared," Joel protested.

"Who got scared tonight?" Jacob teased. "Ha! Ha! Ha!"

That last "Ha! Ha! Ha!" was too much for Noah and Joel. They leaped at Jacob and he raced out the door. They could have spent all night chasing him around the succah if Jacob's mother hadn't called out, "Come in boys! Come into the succah for hot cocoa and cookies."

DO YOU KNOW THAT:

◆ Jews live in thatched huts, called Succot, during this holiday just like their ancestors did when they left Egypt.

◆ The lulav is waved in all directions to show that God is everywhere.

◆ The etrog is a fruit that looks like a lemon.

Mrs. Maccabee Wins the Battle of Hanukkah

Everyone in Modiin agreed that Mrs. Maccabee was a terrible cook. Everyone that is, except Nosher, the family goat.

Mrs. Maccabee made brussels sprouts with whipped cream. She made toasted crickets (the kosher kind) with brown sugar and sweet potatoes. And for dessert she made sugar-covered donuts filled with—cauliflower jelly! The donuts looked delicious, but they made everyone sick. Everyone except Nosher the goat.

Mattityahu (Mr. Maccabee) and the boys—Simon, Judah, Eliezer, Jonathan, and Yohanan didn't want to hurt Mrs. Maccabee's feelings. They ate as much as they could and gave, secretly of course, the left-overs (there were a lot of left-overs) to Nosher. Then they said, "Thank you for dinner, Mama," and went to the felafel stand in Modiin's town square for a snack.

One night Mattityahu and the boys found a crowd of people in the town square. Yossi the felafel man stood in the crowd holding a giant felafel, warm and yummy. On one of Yossi's tables stood a fat soldier wearing a shiny helmet and a short skirt. He was waving his arms and shouting. A line of soldiers stood behind him. They too wore helmets and short skirts. And they were holding mean-looking swords and spears.

"What's happening?" Mattityahu asked Yossi.

"Th-th-the Gr-Gr-Greeks have c-c-come. They're g-g-going to k-k-kill us a-a-all!" Yossi sputtered, shaking in his sandles.

"I command you to bow down to the Greek god Zeus and to bring gifts to the Greek king, Antiochus," shouted the soldier on the table. "If you don't do as I say, we'll kill you all!"

"Yeah!" the soldiers shouted, twirling their spears. "Bow down and bring gifts!"

"Never!" roared Mattityahu. "You can't force us to bow to your god."

But Yossi the felafel man stepped forward. "P-p-please d-d-don't k-k-kill me," he pleaded. "Here's a g-g-gift of a de-de-delicious felafel."

"Meh-eh-eh!" Nosher protested. Felafel was her favorite food. She didn't want Yossi to give it away. Nosher was so angry she butted Yossi. He fell down and the felafel flew up out of his hand. It squished into the face of the fat Greek soldier. Then Mattityahu and the boys jumped on the rest of the surprised soldiers. They grabbed their spears and swords and chased them out of Modiin.

"The Greeks will come back," Mattityahu told the people of Modiin. "Follow me up into the hills. We'll gather a Jewish army to fight the Greeks. We'll *never* bow down to their god. We have only one God!"

Many Jews followed Mattityahu into the hills. But Mrs. Maccabee would not leave her beloved kitchen. Each day Mrs. Maccabee would prepare a basket of food and Nosher would carry it up to the Maccabee army in the hills.

One day there was a sale on cauliflower in the market. Mrs. Maccabee baked a giant batch of cauliflower jelly donuts, the kind that gave everyone bellyaches. Nosher went up the hills holding the handle of the donut-filled basket between her teeth.

As she clip-clopped along she heard the thump of marching feet. She saw helmets shining on the road ahead. It was the Greeks! They were coming back! Nosher dropped the basket of donuts and ran to hide behind some trees. All the donuts spilled out and rolled along the road.

THUMP! THUMP! THUMP! Row after row of Greek soldiers came marching toward Nosher. They were a scary sight with spears held high, flags flying and swords swinging. Suddenly they saw the donuts.

"Homemade donuts!" they cried. "Just like my mother's!"

The soldiers dropped their flags and spears. They spread out, grabbing and gobbling as many donuts as they could.

"Yum, yum, yum..." Nosher could hear the soldiers chewing happily. Then the "Yum, yum, yum" stopped. It got very quiet. Next, Nosher heard, "oooooooh... owww...oooouuch...oooowww!"

"Meh-eh-eh," bleated Nosher. She raced up the hill to call the Maccabees. When Mattityahu and the boys got down to the road the poor Greeks were still rolling on the ground and groaning, "ooooh... owww...oooouuch...oooowww!"

That's how Mrs. Maccabee won the first battle of Hanukkah. And that's why Jews in Israel today eat jelly donuts at their Hanukkah parties—with or without cauliflower.

DO YOU KNOW THAT:

◆ The Greeks didn't want the Jews to believe in God.

◆ Hanukkah means "to dedicate". The Jews threw out all the idols of the Greeks from the Jewish Temple in Jerusalem and re-dedicated the Temple to God.

◆ When the Jews searched for oil for the Temple Menorah they only found a small jar of oil. A miracle happened and the oil in the small jar lasted eight full days. That's why we light eight candles on Hanukkah.

◆ Kids play with a top called a "dreidle" on Hanukkah.

◆ Many Jews eat potato pancakes called "latkes" on Hanukkah.

FIND:
dreidle 1   oil lamp 1
menorah 1   latke 1

THE LITTLE LOST TREE

A truck chugged up a high hill in Israel. It was going to the village of Har Halutz, bringing a load of trees to be planted for Tu B'Shvat—the new year of the trees. Suddenly one sleepy little tree rolled off the back of the truck onto the road.

"Where am I?" cried the tree. "Where are all the other trees? Uh oh! I'm lost!"

At that moment a donkey came strolling along. He nibbled at the grass and pulled at leaves on the roadside as he walked.

"Hee-haw!" he brayed when he saw the tree. "What are you doing here, little tree?"

"I was going to Har Halutz to be planted for Tu B'Shvat, but I fell off the truck. Now I'm lost," the tree said. "I don't know how to get to the village."

"No problem," said the donkey. "I'll take you there." He lifted the tree and held him with his strong, yellow teeth. "Mmmm..." he sniffed the tender, young tree. "You smell delicious. I'll nibble on your branches a bit as we walk."

"No! Don't do that!" cried the little tree. He wiggled and squirmed and tickled the donkey's nose.

"Ah-choo!" sneezed the donkey. He dropped the tree and it quickly rolled off the road into the woods. "Ah-choo!" sneezed the donkey again. He looked around. "Where did that delicious tree go?" he thought.

The little tree hugged his branches tightly and stayed very quiet. The donkey looked and looked, but there were so many trees in the forest he couldn't see the little tree. Finally, the donkey walked on, nibbling grass as he went.

A gust of wind raced through the woods. Whoosh! It blew the tree into a clearing where a boy and girl were making a campfire.

"Who are you?" they asked him.

"I'm a Tu B'Shvat tree. I feel off a truck on the way to Har Halutz and now I'm lost. I'll never be planted in time for Tu B'Shvat."

"Tch, tch, tch," said the boy and girl. "Don't be sad. We live near Har Halutz. We'll take you there as soon as we toast our marshmallows. We just need a little more wood for the fire. Could we have one of your little branches?"

"Let go!" yelled the tree.

He kicked with his roots and rolled himself out of the clearing. He rolled and rolled until he bumped against a big gray rock. Now he felt safe, but very sad and tired. Sadly and tiredly the tree fell asleep.

Suddenly something wet trickled over his lowest leaves. "What's that?" wondered the tree. "It can't be raining on just some of my leaves."

A small spotted dog stood beside him. "Oh, excuse me," woofed the dog shyly. "I just watered you. I hope you don't mind."

"You hope I don't mind!" cried the little tree. "First I fell off the truck. Then a donkey nearly ate me. Then a boy and girl almost put me into their campfire. And now you wet me. This is the worst day in my life! I'll never get to Har Halutz. I'll never get planted!"

The little tree was so miserable that he wanted to cry—only he didn't know how.

"Calm down," said the spotted dog. "I don't eat trees and I don't make fires with trees. I just water them. And Har Halutz has lots of dogs, so it always needs more trees."

He gently lifted the little tree and trotted through the woods. When they reached the village the people were getting ready to plant for Tu B'Shvat.

"Hurray!" they cheered. "Here's another tree to plant. Good dog!" They patted the small spotted dog.

The people dug a hole for the little tree. They piled earth carefully around his roots and sprinkled water on him. The water cooled and tickled the tree. He drank and drank. He waved his branches happily and thought, "This started out as the worst day in my life—but now it's the best day. I'm not lost anymore. I'm home!"

DO YOU KNOW THAT:

◆ Tu B'Shvat means the 15th day of the Hebrew month of Shvat.

◆ Trees are very important in Israel not only for food but also for shade and to help keep the soil healthy.

◆ On Tu B'Shvat Jews in Israel go all across the country to plant new trees.

◆ The Jewish National Fund (JNF) collects money to plant trees in Israel. Children like you, and their families, have helped plant millions of trees in Israel.

◆ Jews all over the world make a special point of eating the fruits of trees grown in Israel on Tu B'Shvat.

FIND:

cherries 4
watering can 1
rose 2

A Purim Thank-You Dish

Jeremy's mother baked all morning on the day before Purim. The table was covered with fruit tarts, almond cookies, cinnamon buns, honey cake and many more goodies. Jeremy's mother packed dishes of treats and covered each with a white napkin.

"Please, please Mom, can I have one little cookie?" Jeremy begged.

"First you'll deliver these dishes for me, then you can eat. One to Grandma, one to Aunt Esther, and this big one to my best friend, Hannah. She always sends me such a nice, full dish at Purim."

"But Mom! I'm hungry!" Jeremy wailed.

"So walk fast. But don't run. Don't drop anything and don't fall. Just knock on the door, say 'Happy Purim. Here's a dish of Purim treats for you.' And if they give you some money say, 'Thank you very much.'"

Jeremy's mother wrapped his scarf around his neck, plopped his cap on his head, handed him the three Purim dishes and pushed him out the door.

"Happy Purim. Here's a dish of Purim treats for you. Thank you very much. Happy Purim. Here's a dish..." Jeremy repeated to himself as he walked. He got to Grandma's house without dropping anything.

"Happy thank you, here's a Purim of dish treats, thank you very much," he mumbled. Grandma laughed, kissed him on the nose and dropped a coin in his pocket.

The sweet smell of cookies and the tangy smell of oranges made Jeremy's mouth water. He wished he could have one tiny little taste! Somehow, he got to Aunt Esther's without even peeking under the napkin.

"Thank-you-Purim-here's-a-treat-happy... uh...happy-dishes," he squeezed out the words so fast his aunt couldn't even understand what he was saying.

"Thank you, Jeremy," she smiled. She pinched his cheek and dropped a coin in his pocket.

All he had left now was the last, biggest dish to bring to his mother's best friend, Hannah. Her house was right in the middle of town. Jeremy was almost running by now. Turning a corner, he bumped into Hannah's son, Avi. Avi was carrying a big covered dish, too.

"Where are you going?" asked Jeremy.

"To your house," answered Avi. "Where are *you* going?"

"To your house," said Jeremy.

"What've you got?" Avi wanted to know.

"If you show me, I'll show you," Jeremy answered.

They put their dishes down on the newspaper stand in front of Mr. Goldstein's candy store and lifted the napkins. Each dish had two large oranges, four different cookies, raisins, walnuts, and three kinds of cake. They were perfectly matched.

"Mmmmmm..." Jeremy licked his lips. "If I take one of your brownies no one will notice, right?"

"Right," answered Avi. "And if I take two of your date cookies to even things up, no one will notice, right?"

They crunched and munched for a minute.

"How about a piece of honey cake?" offered Jeremy.

"Sure. Here's a piece of sponge cake." Avi handed him the cake.

"Want an orange?" Jeremy suggested.

"Why not?" Avi smiled, handing Jeremy his orange. "As long as we keep it even."

Jeremy and Avi finally finished. They wiped the crumbs off their mouths and went off to deliver their dishes.

"Happy treat, here's a Purim thank-you dish," Jeremy said cheerfully when Hannah opened her door.

"Thank you, Jeremy," she said and lifted the napkin. Her face turned red. "What—it's almost empty!" she screamed. "Such an insult! This is a slap in the face! Why, I never heard of such chutzpah! Is this how she treats her best friend? I'll never speak to your mother again!"

Jeremy turned and ran home. He found his mother yelling, "Hannah is laughing at me, insulting me with a half-empty dish. I'll never speak to her again!"

That might have been the sad end of the story. But luckily, Mr. Goldstein, the owner of the candy store, saw Jeremy and Avi exchanging Purim treats. He told Jeremy's father, who told Jeremy's mother, who rushed to Hannah's house to tell her. The friends laughed and hugged and made up.

And then two things happened to Jeremy and Avi. First, they got punished. And second, they got tummy aches.

DO YOU KNOW THAT:

◆ The word "purim" means lottery.

◆ Megillat Esther is read on Purim. It is a long scroll of parchment that looks like paper. The reader folds the pages of the Megillah to make it look like a book or a letter.

◆ Megillat Esther tells about Ahashverosh, King of Persia, and how Haman, his wicked advisor, tried to kill the Jews. Esther, the King's Jewish wife, found out what Haman wanted to do. With the help of Mordechai, the leader of the Jews, she saved the Jewish people.

◆ On Purim, Jews give presents of food, called Shalach Manot, to their friends and neighbors.

◆ Children bang their feet and twirl noisemakers, called groggers, whenever they hear the wicked Haman's name. Some kids even fire cap pistols and shout "Booooooo!".

FIND:

hamantaschen 2
Megillat Esther 2
grogger 1

GOLDSTEIN'S

SIMPLE SIMON'S SEDER

Kids have a lot to do at a Passover Seder. They have to read the Haggadah (or at least look at the pictures), eat the big Seder meal, open the door for Elijah, and stay up until very late into the night.

But the most important thing kids have to do at a Seder is ask the Four Questions—the Mah Nishtanah—and, of course, hide the Afikoman.

Simon was almost the youngest child at his Seder. His baby brother was only two years old. So it was Simon who had to ask the Four Questions at the Seder.

All his cousins—David, Josh and Judy— liked to tease him. "Hey Simple Simon, think you can remember *all* the Four Questions? We hope they're not too *complicated* for you."

Simon got angry. "Don't call me simple!" he yelled.

When Simon stood on the chair to ask the Four Questions his knees were shaking inside his new corduroy pants. The whole family was watching. Even his cousins.

"Mah Nishtanah Halaylah Hazeh..." he began. To his surprise, it was easy. The first two questions went as smoothly as ice cream. But on the third question Simon started to stutter.

"Uh...Sheh...sheh...b...chol...ha...ha..."

"Gesundheit!" Josh yelled, pretending Simon had sneezed. Then all his cousins giggled. "Poor Simple Simon," they sang. "Poor simple, simple Simon."

Simon looked down at his shoes, but he didn't cry.

Suddenly, his grandma began to sing along softly, "Sheh b'chol halaylot ayn anoo matbeeleem...." Simon lifted his head. All at once he remembered the words. In a flash, he finished saying all the Four Questions.

"Thanks, Grandma," he whispered as he sat down.

When David, the oldest cousin, stole the afikoman, Simon wanted to help hide it. But David said, "You'd only think of a simple place where anyone could find it."

Simon stuck his tongue out at him.

"Don't be upset," whispered Grandma, who saw everything. "Sometimes the simplest way is the best way."

Simon tried hard not to feel bad. He looked at the Haggadah pictures and pretended to be happy. He fed slices of apple to his little brother. Then he helped clear the table for the meal. And when everyone had finished eating, he helped bring the Haggadahs, the Seder dish, and the big matzo dish back to the table.

"Now we'll eat the afikoman and finish our Seder," Grandpa announced. "Come on children," he coaxed, "where's the afikoman?"

David, Josh and Judy smiled proudly. They were thinking about the presents they were going to get for giving back the afikoman.

"I have it," David said. He reached into the bookcase. But there was no afikoman inside.

Josh started to laugh. "It was too easy to find in the bookcase," he said. "So I took it and hid it behind the rocking chair."

He bent to get it. But there was no afikoman behind the rocking chair.

Now Judy started to laugh. "Anyone could see it behind the rocking chair," she told them. "So I put it under grandma's coat." She went over and looked under the coat on the couch, but there was nothing there.

"Oh yes," grandma said. "I thought I saw a wrapped piece of matzo over there, so I put it away."

"Where?" all the cousins asked excitedly.

Grandma tapped her forehead. "Now where, where did I put it? Let me think... hmmm.... Ah yes, I'm beginning to remember. I put it where matzo ought to be." And she winked at Simon.

"Where should matzo be?" everyone asked.

"In the matzo box!" David yelled, as he ran to look on the shelf.

"In the oven!" exclaimed Judy, as she bent down to look.

"In the chicken soup?" wondered Mother, as she peeked into the pot of left-over soup.

"Where *should* matzo be?" wondered Simon out loud.

And then he laughed. Of course. It was so simple.

"Here it is!" he exclaimed, lifting the cover from the matzo dish on the table. And there was the afikoman.

"Of course," said Grandma. "It was simple." Smiling, she turned to David, Josh and Judy. "I know you like to make fun of Simon," she said. "But while you were running around and looking for hard places where the afikoman might be hidden, Simon found it right away. That's because he thinks in a clear and simple way."

Simon was proud of himself.

He was even a little sorry that his baby brother might be asking the Four Questions next year instead of him.

DO YOU KNOW THAT:

◆ The word "afikoman" means dessert.

◆ The Haggadah tells the story of how and why the Jewish people left Egypt.

◆ It is the custom to eat matzo and drink wine at the Seder while leaning to your left side.

◆ Matzo is bread that is not allowed to rise (get thick).

FIND

matzo
frog
locus

The Curious Queen

Asmaru hated to say good-bye to her chickens, her white goat, and her round, straw-roofed house. But she had to do it because her family and all the other Jewish families in the village were moving to Israel.

"Why?" Asmaru asked her older sister, Hami. "Why should we leave Ethiopia and go to a far-away land?"

Her big sister smiled. "It's because we had a very beautiful, very curious great, great, great, great-grandmother," she said. "Sit here and help me pick the pebbles out of these beans and I'll tell you about our long-ago grandmother— the Queen of Sheba."

Asmaru sat down. She hated sorting beans, but she needed an answer to her question.

Then Hami began:

Once, our land Ethiopia was called the Land of Sheba. The ruler of Sheba was a beautiful queen. Her skin was the color of cinnamon, just like yours. She wore a long white gown with jewels along the hem, and she wore pearls in her curly black hair. The queen ruled over a thousand cities. She thought she was the strongest ruler in the world.

One day, a trader from far away lands came to her palace. He told her about Solomon, the king of the Land of Israel.

"Solomon," he said, "is so wise that he can speak the languages of the birds and animals. He can solve any riddle and make wise decisions on any problem."

"That's impossible," thought the queen. "But I'm curious. I have to see for myself."

The queen loaded five-hundred camels with gifts for King Solomon. She took baskets of spices, cages of brightly colored parrots and peacocks, gold and silver dishes, a family of monkeys and three brown lion cubs. Then she started on the long trip to Israel.

King Solomon came to meet the Queen of Sheba when she reached Jerusalem, Israel's capital. She saw that he was tall and very handsome with his purple robe, long curly beard, and bright blue eyes. And he thought she was beautiful with her cinnamon-colored skin, white robe, and black hair wound 'round with pearls. They sat in the garden and the queen's servants carried in the gifts she had brought. As soon as the lion cubs were brought in they began to yowl. King Solomon sat down on the grass beside them. He and the cubs began to yelp to each other. Then he said to the queen, "Please send these cubs home. They're too young. They miss their mother."

"So it's true that Solomon can speak the languages of animals," thought the queen. "Can he also answer riddles?"

She asked him, "Wise king, please tell me: What is not born, does not die, and lives forever?"

The king answered right away. "The Lord our God."

Then the Queen of Sheba called in fifty boys and girls. They all had short hair, were dressed in the same white robes, and looked exactly alike.

"Which of these children are boys and which are girls?" she asked the king.

King Solomon asked his servants to bring in a table loaded with fruits and candies.

"Please help yourselves," he said to the children.

Twenty-five of the children rushed forward to eat. The others waited shyly to be asked again.

"The first twenty-five are the boys," declared the king.

Now, at last, the queen's curiosity was satisfied.

Not long after, King Solomon and the Queen of Sheba were married. They settled down in his palace and spent many happy weeks and months to-gether. They even wrote poems to each other and to God. We still read some of King Solomon's poems at Passover time.

After a while, the queen gave birth to a beautiful baby. And then it was time for her to go home. The king kissed the baby for the last time. And the queen took the baby back to the Land of Sheba.

"Did the king and queen ever see each other again?" asked Asmaru.

"Never," Hami answered. "But all of us, all the Jews of Ethiopia, are the great, great, great-grandchildren of King Solomon and the Queen of Sheba's baby."

Asmaru thought about the story as she finished sorting the beans. "That means Israel is also my country, just like Ethiopia is my country," she said after awhile. "I guess I'll go. I hope we'll have goats and chickens in Israel, like we have here."

"Maybe," said her big sister. She stood up and brushed her skirt. "And maybe we'll even have fruits and candies," she smiled.

DO YOU KNOW THAT:

◆ Ethiopia is a country in Africa.

◆ Ethiopian Jews have their own rabbis called "Kessim".

◆ Most of the Ethiopian Jews now live in Israel.

◆ King Solomon built The Second Temple in Jerusalem. It had enough room inside for thousands of people to pray to God.

◆ On Passover, Jews read King Solomon's Shir Hashirim, The Song of Songs, in the synagogue.

A Birthday Present for the Torah

We're having a birth-day party this week," announced Mrs. Plotkin, the Sunday School teacher.

"Who's birthday is it?" asked Shira.

"It's the Torah's birthday. God gave the Torah to the Jewish people on Shavuot, the holiday we celebrate this Tuesday. It's a springtime holiday. On Shavuot, Jews would come to the Temple in Jerusalem bringing baskets filled with the first fruits of their fields."

Davy, Shira, Jon and Abby thought about the Torah's birthday as they walked home.

"We ought to give the Torah a present," Shira suggested.

"Is the Torah a boy or a girl?" Jon asked.

"What difference does that make?" Abby wanted to know.

"Well, boys and girls get different kinds of presents," Jon explained.

"That's silly," Abby argued. "Skates and Legos and tennis balls and sweatshirts are the same for boys and girls."

"Can you see our Torah in skates and a sweatshirt," Davy laughed. "But let's think... What can we get the Torah for its birthday?"

"A birthday cake!" Jon said, smacking his lips. "With chocolate icing and sprinkles and cherries."

"You're too funny. Torahs can't eat," declared Shira. "But I have an idea. Our Torah in the synagogue has a purple velvet cover with gold embroidery. But it's very old. We could make a new cover. My mom has some soft pink velvet we can use."

"And we have gold trim in our sewing box at home," offered Abby.

"We could sew glass beads and little gold bells on the cover, too," Davy added.

"It'll be beautiful!" Shira declared, and clapped her hands.

After lunch, Shira spread a blanket on the soft, new grass. Bounder, the big brown dog from next door barked a friendly "hello."

"We can't play now, Bounder," called Shira. "We're busy."

Everyone had brought material to start making the cover. They cut the velvet and sewed the ends together. Then they sewed red, yellow and blue beads all over. Davy brought some tinkling gold bells from his crafts box. They sewed them along the top. And last of all, Jon and Abby held the trim in place while Davy and Shira glued it down on the soft pink velvet. When they finished, they stepped back to look. The cover was a little crooked—but it was beautiful!

Jon pulled a bag of squashed potato chips out of his pocket. "Let's eat while the glue dries," he said. They sat on the grass near the vegetable garden and shared potato chips.

"Look," Shira pointed. "There are red strawberries in the strawberry patch."

"And tiny green pods on the pea plant," Jon exclaimed. "Hey—Mrs. Plotkin told us that Shavuot was also the holiday of the first fruits."

"That means this Tuesday is the birthday of the Torah *and* the first fruits?" Abby asked.

"Sort of," Jon answered. Their teacher had never really said it was a fruit birthday.

"Arf, arf," Bounder barked from the yard next door. He poked his wet black nose through the bushes. He wanted to play.

"Stay out!" shouted Shira. "Out!"

But it was too late. Bounder sprang happily into the yard. He grabbed the Torah cover in his teeth and ran, begging the children to chase him. Around and around the yard they ran—Bounder and the flapping pink cover, with Shira, Jon, Abby and Davy running after him, yelling, "Stop! Help! Let go!"

Shira grabbed one end of the cover. The children heard a R-I-I-I-P! Then Bounder dropped it and galloped out of the yard. Shira held up the torn cover. It had tooth marks, paw marks, dirt marks and an awful rip down the middle. It was ruined.

"Now what'll we do?" Shira groaned. They all sat down sadly around the ruined cover. Abby patted the soft velvet and sniffled. Pink apple blossoms floated down on their heads.

Suddenly Davy yelled, "I have a great idea! Let's bring our first fruits to the Torah. We can bring little new peas and red strawberries and lots of other fruits and vegetables. That way the Torah and the fruits can celebrate their birthdays together."

"Fantastic," Shira cried. "I have a straw basket we can use."

Abby jumped up, holding the pink velvet. "I'll clean the velvet and we can put it in the bottom of the basket," she said. "It'll be so pretty!"

"First fruits," Jon smiled happily, patting his stomach. He picked a strawberry from the strawberry patch.

"Happy birthday little first strawberry," he said.

"Happy birthday," all the children joined in.

DO YOU KNOW THAT:

◆ The word "shavuot" means weeks. There are seven weeks between Passover—when the Jews left Egypt—and Shavuot.

◆ The Torah was given to the Jews on Mt. Sinai in Israel.

◆ Moses brought down the Ten Commandments after spending 40 days on Mt. Sinai.

◆ "Blintzes" are cheese-filled crepes that Jews eat on Shavuot.

In Faraway Places*

In the days of the Bible a great, shining Temple stood in Jerusalem in the land of Judea. Its outside walls were covered with layers of gleaming gold and it had giant gates all around. Golden menorahs and incense burners, carved tables and washing basins filled the rooms. And bright draperies warmed the stone walls.

This was a special Temple, for the angels of heaven watched over it. They loved to watch the Jewish people celebrate their holidays in the Temple. On Succot, Passover, and Shavuot people came to the Holy Temple from all over the land of Judea, and from other lands as well. They led donkeys and oxen wearing olive branch necklaces and carrying gifts for God.

The angels smiled as the Levites sang praises to God and all the people sang along. The golden trumpets of the musicians blared, bells jingled, and harps rippled. The people prayed and danced and visited with friends. The children played hide-and-seek between the market stalls.

One day, an enemy army marched into Judea. The enemy soldiers smashed the small army of the Jews and marched on to the walls of Jerusalem and the Temple. Many of the people of the city were frightened and ran away. Others stayed to fight.

From the Temple walls the Jews shot arrows, threw spears and dropped heavy rocks on the soldiers. They fought for many months. But at last, on the ninth day of the Jewish month of Av—in the heat of the summer—the enemy broke down the Temple gates. The enemy soldiers raced through the rooms with burning torches and set fire to the draperies and everything inside. Soon all of the Holy Temple was on fire.

The flames roared and poked hot fingers into the sky. High in the heavens the horrified angels saw the Temple burning. They swooped down and beat the flames with their wings. But the fire roared on. Then each angel lifted one of the blackened stones from the burning walls. They carried the stones far away from Judea. In each land that they passed the angels dropped a stone.

"We'll leave these stones here for safekeeping," they said. "On the day that the Jews begin to build their Temple again, the stones will be returned to Jerusalem."

Once their Temple was destroyed, the Jews of Judea were forced to leave their land. They wandered far over the deserts, mountains and seas. And to their wonder, in faraway lands, they found the stones of the Temple.

In each place that the Jews found a Temple stone they built a synagogue. They prayed, celebrated holidays and sang in their new synagogues. But they never forgot their Holy Temple in Jerusalem.

Every year on the ninth day of the Jewish month of Av—the very day the Temple was destroyed—they would ask God to help them rebuild their Temple. The adults would not eat or drink for a whole day. The children would feel sad too.

And when they looked at the blackened Temple stone in their synagogue wall they remembered what the angels had done.

"This stone was only given to us to keep for awhile," the Jews said. "When it's time to rebuild the Temple in Jerusalem we'll return it to its place in the Temple wall."

*Based on a Midrash (A Jewish Legend)

DO YOU KNOW THAT:

◆ Both the First and the Second Temples were destroyed on Tisha B'Av (9th day of Av).

◆ On Tisha B'Av, many Jews sit on the hard ground, even in the synagogue, to remember how hard life was when the Temples were destroyed.

◆ In the synagogue, very sad poems are read. These poems tell about what happened to the people in Jerusalem. Fathers and mothers sometimes cry when they read these poems.

◆ People don't even say hello to each other on Tisha B'Av.

◆ The Kotel, which means "wall" in Hebrew, is all that remains from the Second Temple. If you ever visit Israel you can go to The Kotel and see how big the stones are.

◆ In Israel, thousands of Jews go to The Kotel on Tisha B'Av to ask God to help them build The Third Temple.

MUTTLEY'S FIRST SHABBAT

Mrs. Kugel loved dogs. But today, Muttley, the family's new cocker spaniel, was constantly getting in the way.

"Get out from under my feet, Muttley! I'm cleaning up for Shabbat," she scolded. SWISH! She gently swept him out the kitchen door into the backyard. BANG! The door slammed shut.

Muttley picked himself up and shook himself up and down and sideways. "What's all the fuss about? What's special about Shabbat?" he grumbled.

A brown chipmunk with fat cheeks ran past. "What's special about Shabbat?" she chattered. "Good food is what's special. I always save my biggest acorns for Shabbat dinner."

Muttley licked his whiskers. He sniffed the delicious smell of challah baking in the oven. "She's right," he said. "Shabbat means good food."

Suddenly a shower of egg shells, leaves and twigs fell onto his head. FFFMMFF! Muttley sneezed and snuffled. Then he looked up. A red robin was sweeping out her nest right above him. "What's special about Shabbat?" she chirped. "A clean house is what's special about Shabbat."

Muttley shook a piece of shell off his nose. He thought of the broom that swept him out of the house. "She's right," he said. "Shabbat means good food *and* a clean house."

"What's special about Shabbat?" mewed three gray and white kittens from the next yard. Their mother was licking their ears and backs and bellies till their fur was shiny clean. "A bath is what's special about Shabbat," they purred.

Brrr..Muttley's nose quivered. "They're right. I had a bath today too. So Shabbat means good food, a clean house *and* a bath."

Just then a white mouse scurried between Muttley's legs. The mouse stopped at his front door-hole under a rose bush. "What's special about Shabbat?" he squeaked. "On Shabbat I invite company to share my dinner." Suddenly, all over the garden mice popped out of their holes. "We're coming," they announced.

"Can I come too?" asked Muttley. "Tee, hee, hee," the mice giggled. "Don't be silly." And into the door-hole they scurried.

Muttley looked around. The chipmunk, the sparrow, the kittens and all the mice were gone. Dark shadows filled the yard. Muttley was lonely.

"Shabbat means good food, a clean house, a bath, *and* company for dinner. But Mrs. Kugel chased me out and here I am, alone," he sniffed sadly, feeling sorry for himself. Then he pointed his nose up and began to howl. "Owwww...wwww."

Suddenly a little spotted puppy wriggled through the fence. "I'm alone too," he whimpered.

Muttley sniffed the puppy and the puppy sniffed Muttley. Then they snuggled close together, pointed their noses at the setting sun, and howled. "Owwwww...wwwww."

The kitchen door opened. "Muttley!" Mrs. Kugel called. "Stop that howling and come in. It's time to light the Shabbat candles."

"Yippee! Yip," Muttley yelped happily. He jumped up and raced across the yard and up the steps.

"Owwww...wwww" howled the spotted puppy left all by himself in the yard.

Muttley stopped. He looked back at the puppy. "How can I leave him alone on Shabbat," he thought. He shook himself up and down and sideways and thought again.

"The white mouse was right. On Shabbat we're supposed to invite company. I'll invite the puppy for Shabbat dinner!"

But then he had another thought, a sad thought. It made his ears droop like banana peels. "Maybe my new family doesn't know about inviting company on Shabbat. They may sweep us both out the door."

"Owwww...wwww", the puppy howled, louder than ever. Muttley made a brave decision.

"Woof! Woof!" he called to the puppy. "Come with me."

The puppy jumped for joy and scampered up the steps and into the house.

Muttley and his new friend smelled the good food and saw the candlesticks, challah, and wine on the table. Around the table stood Muttley's new family, scrubbed and smiling. There were two people standing right near Mr. Kugel. "Shabbat guests!" thought Muttley.

Everyone was waiting for Muttley so they could light the Shabbat candles.

The youngest child pointed to the spotted puppy. "Look," she said, "Muttley invited company for Shabbat dinner just like we did. What a smart dog."

"Woof! Woof!" Muttley barked happily. "What a smart family," he thought, and he wagged his tail up and down and sideways as hard as he could.

DO YOU KNOW THAT:

◆ "Kugel" is a kind of noodle pie that Jews eat on Shabbat.

◆ The most popular song sung on Shabbat is "Shalom Aleichem", welcoming the Shabbat Angels.

◆ There is a special Shabbat song to honor mothers called "Ayshet Chayil".

◆ In Israel a siren blares throughout the whole country to announce the arrival of Shabbat.